Josh grew up in Derbyshire in the United Kingdom with his mother, father and younger sister. He lived a lavish life partying and studying in tandem. He is an alumnus of the University of Nottingham where he would move to with his childhood sweetheart Jenny. He worked as a registered nurse full time for five years. During this period of affluence, he began using opioids which spiralled into an addiction to heroin, benzodiazepines and cocaine. Unable to maintain addiction and nursing, he lost his dream job and headed for destruction. At 27, he recovered from addiction and graduated as a barber. He kept journals throughout; this is his journey from professional to addict and survivor. He now resides with his much-loved fiancée Jenny and Cat Diekin, his soulmates scars and all.

Joshua Bullock

THE CRUISE VACATION

From Nurse to
Junky to Barber

AUSTIN MACAULEY PUBLISHERS™
LONDON • CAMBRIDGE • NEW YORK • SHARJAH

Copyright © Joshua Bullock 2023

The right of Joshua Bullock to be identified as author of this work has been asserted by the author in accordance with sections 77 and 78 of the Copyright, Designs and Patents Act 1988.

All rights reserved. No part of this publication may be reproduced, stored in a retrieval system, or transmitted in any form or by any means, electronic, mechanical, photocopying, recording, or otherwise, without the prior permission of the publishers.

Any person who commits any unauthorised act in relation to this publication may be liable to criminal prosecution and civil claims for damages.

This is a work of fiction. Names, characters, businesses, places, events, locales, and incidents are either the products of the author's imagination or used in a fictitious manner. Any resemblance to actual persons, living or dead, or actual events is purely coincidental.

A CIP catalogue record for this title is available from the British Library.

ISBN 9781398475526 (Paperback)
ISBN 9781398475533 (ePub e-book)

www.austinmacauley.com

First Published 2023
Austin Macauley Publishers Ltd®
1 Canada Square
Canary Wharf
London
E14 5AA

I would like to thank foremost, my fiancé, childhood sweetheart – Jenny. Not only would I be completely lost inside my beat-up old mind, but I would be dead and unable to share my work. I would like to thank my sister Meghan, my nieces Ava and Dotty, my father Dexter, his partner Lee and my beautifully sweet and resolute mother Lisa for guiding me best they can and teaching me how to enjoy life with clarity and sobriety. Thank you, Kev, from the bottom of my heart for all the good times shared and in advance all the good times to come, thank you, brother. Thank you to Emma for your lifelong friendship and dance partner. A big thank you goes out to Luke, a partner in crime, for all the good times and for not giving up on me; must have been hard. Much love to my entire friendship group I'm still lucky to have. I cannot thank you enough. You know who you are. One love.

My work is greatly influenced by the writings of the late William S Burroughs, post World War two. The excess of morphine and its derivates spread throughout New York's newfound, thrilling underground through to Paris – the "French connection" and arriving on to the UK Shores. Bill's writing is unapologetically stark and true to his word. The late Jack Kerouac I have to thank for his prose in writing especially recognisable in his novel *On the Road* – poetic and free thinking. Irvine Welsh is a great example of a modern-day Beatnik author, seeking out fun, stumbling on drug use and struggling through life harmoniously. Thank you for your comfort in the words you have written – I have read your work and reread them all to remember how it's done. I thank all those blues artists out there, all those cats playing their guitars to warm me up, techno mixed and played to the masses by a founding father of German dance, Sven Vath Keeping that beat pumping and me dancing – happy, content, utter escapism. Alexander Trocchi's *Cain's Book*; Hubert Sellby Jr's *Last Exit to Brooklyn*, and Herbert Huncke's collective writings have all had an immense impact on my lifestyle, experiences, for good or for ill, ultimately injecting me with the confidence that enabled me to tell my story as is.

The late and great Hunter S Thompson; the American Journalist, Sports writer, Novelist and the creator of what he coined "Gonzo Journalism" encouraged my voyeurism in writing as well as considering words and prose as a form of music continues to have profound resonation in my work, including humour, dark humour and vulgarity which at times I believe require a daring idol to expand on to gain confidence and to continue in his footsteps.

To all those beatniks along the way I could have included, your writing is apparent in my work.

I would like to say a huge thank you to my fiancé and life partner Jenny Whittle Bullock for choosing to devote and dedicate her precious time to stand by my side through my hardships and work with me in painting the artwork for the cover of The Cruise Vacation. Your artwork encapsulates the horrifying hell and crudity of drug use and addiction. Jenny stood by my side while I was strung out on dope; sick, tired and beat. Her art, although simple, illustrates what addicts crave to the point of death perfectly. The horror and waste of life I choose for over ten years. The art orates what my world revolved around every hour of every day of every month of every year where I spent comfortably numb, unconscious and a slave to the ugly entity of smack and the connections feeding the gorilla on my back.

The fine art reminds me of the absolute ugliness of the junk which I pumped around my circulatory system oh-so-willingly until I closed in on death. Without Jenny Whittle Bullock, I wouldn't have been here to write the book you hold today. The significance of the artwork is a constant reminder to me of the poisons I used to escape life and take the easy way out of living. How selfish of me. Junk is an illusion – no happiness to be find here man…

My courtesy goes out to my publisher Austin McCauley for recreating Jenny's artwork to enable its use on my book cover. Huge respect to these guys, they may have just saved countless lives in my opinion. It's an aggressively nasty piece of art that is all too familiar an image for too many people world over. Its ugliness is stark and aggressive – something kool cats will dig and understand. Live on beautiful people.

"But what can eternity of damnation matter to someone who has felt, if only for a second, the infinity of delight" ~Charles Baudelaire.

By Joshua Bullock, recovered drug addict, nurse and now getting by as a level 3 advanced barber.

Chapter 1
In the Old Toad Boozer

When a man is junk sick and having procured his fix, the mix of excitement, desperation and relief is a kick in of itself. I pick up the wrap and rush swiftly to a location where I can take a hit. Pub toilets were a frequent choice no matter of their disrepair or grandeur. I would line out the brown crumbled rocks and powder on a smooth surface, usually my bank card balanced precariously on top of the paper dispenser, and rack up two decent sized lines. I would then clear up my instruments and wrap the remaining junk up to stash before focusing my attention on the lines.

Before my fix I would have sweat covering my back and collar. My legs would ache and my skin felt sharp and dirty. I would struggle to hold the contents of my bowel in and the stomach pain was intensifying in waves. What I hated the most was my streaming, dilated eyes that were sensitive and uncomfortable. I would shiver cold with hot flashes as I loomed over the two brown lines I had cut.

My mouth would salivate and I'd be overcome with reassuring warmth that my fix was imminent. I'd twitch with excitement while swallowing some bile as the sickness grew worse. I shake uncontrollably. "Now is the time to fix".

A new sense of urgency panics me into hurrying as two old timers enter the toilet while talking about one's recent cruise around the Caribbean. Their voices are exaggerated; sharp and threatening. It's almost like they know that behind the stall, hard narcotics are being prepared. Heroin lay out awaiting consumption. A stark and intriguing contrast to their pints of ale they have settling at the bar. My hands become clammy. I look back down at the two lines and roll up a bus ticket quickly. I shook with nervous energy exacerbating the sickness further.

A fleeting feeling of guilt ran over me as I acknowledged my horrendous condition and the powder that would land me in withdrawals should my supply be cut off. Nobody forced me into addiction. It just seemed a perfect remedy at the time, the drug that is. After all, junk allows for confidence, disinhibits you not to care about the petty and hurtful and in the words of Lou Reed of The Velvet Underground "*It makes me feel like a man*". Which is all very appealing to most I would imagine, only I was the man to take the initiative to remedy the plight. By this I mean remedy one's perception of the complications in life or more accurately, the feelings of negativity and lack of self-confidence that has hindered me since I was a boy of school age. Initiative is usually commended and encouraged and battles do not rage on without suffering. Here I am suffering greatly and my medication is in two rails of light tan brown powder.

My mouth waters uncontrollably as I snort one line of heroin up each nostril, lightly sniffing so to ensure optimum position of the junk up the nose. We are aiming for capillaries, arteries and veins.

Chapter 2
The Boy Who Knew Better

The feeling of anxiety I had begun experiencing years ago around the age of eleven or twelve, had symptoms primarily of surplus energy but also desperation to be regarded by my peers as cool and by my father, as successful and a perfect fit into a square society. My mother is generally more liberal. At secondary school I once threw a milkshake through the staff room window landing unintentionally in my history teacher's lap while apparently, she ate her lunch. She came to afternoon class in biking gear minus the helmet. She rode her bike to school, a good job too. I would make devices that would send pencils flying across the room causing class wide disruption and for me, satisfaction. I meant no malice while doing such things and unbeknown to most I think, I was actually paying attention in class. It was basically secondary school tomfoolery. I did not fail school quite the opposite. I would say with this surplus energy, that hyperactivity is an accurate description of my behaviour and I'm sure my parents would most certainly agree. A cock sure need to entertain like some sort of theatrical performer for my peers, it excited me despite my actions landing me in bother most of the time.

Roll by a couple of years and I would discover the delicious delights of the vine-alcohol. Alcohol was an excellent discovery for me and one grandfathered in by my family, friends and folk on a daily basis. My parents were hard working and rather well functioning and intermittent alcoholics. But is it not every man who has a taste for the hop? It is well established I think, that few people go to a boozer for just the one spiked drink. It is just not the nature of going down the pub or that's what I personally found anyhow. Moreover, "just the one" is not a characteristic of the drug of the grape. Alcohol, much like cocaine and *methadrone is rather moreish especially once intoxication takes hold and it does not take much drink to achieve a kick much like its counterparts – drugs. I grew up around booze so it was a social normality in my eyes. Drink would calm my otherwise wired head space and lull me into a mood of fluidity, confidence and pleasure – sometimes luring me into petty trouble and frankly turning me into a walking liability. Friday evenings after school we would (after procuring our booze from our elders), terrorise our local quaint village by playing mostly harmless albeit annoying pranks. This, I think, was the handle. It was the handle to the door to mind alteration, adrenaline manipulation and experimentation for good and for ill.

It was not until a while later on in my life, subsequent to experiences with mind alteration primarily caused by alcohol experimentation, when I began mixing booze with a substance used for worming animals called Benzylpiperazine. I must attempt to explore this later as I feel its relevance resonates as my story unfolds. Suffice to say, Benzylpiperazine is a drug which holds similar properties to amphetamines and generally provides that sought after euphoria folk have chased through the centuries.

So, with alcohol being a top shelver, a staple intoxicant, it fuelled my curiosity immeasurably. I can still imagine feeling the neurons lighting up my mind. Synapses firing and excitement, "YES". What can this brain I have actually do? What is this body capable of? What is my mind capable of? How can I feel? As it turns out, a lot has been learnt on my journey. Mostly learnt the hard way but learnt and implemented nonetheless. The animal worming medicine showed me at least, the power of euphoria if only it stuck around for a few hours. I would drop a few donkey choking caps of the stuff. The big bastards rolling over my tongue and down the gullet always triggering retching and a taste I have since forgotten but remember to be foul and that drinks close by would be highly preferable.

Me and some close friends; Joe, Stu, Tyler and Francesca would commute to the local town of Chesterfield straight out of school on a Thursday or Friday evening to score the caps. We also experimented a lot with LSA extracted from the small seeds of the Hawaiian Wood rose bush. We would get down to some music and dance around like court jesters. Kissing and hugging one another. I remember the trips to be positive experiences, the only downside to the Baby wood rose seeds was the nausea that peaked early and faded albeit gradually. They always had the tendency to send the stomach into turmoil causing nausea and vomiting but it rarely ruined my trip. I was happily intoxicated. I had not long turned fifteen. I felt like I had happened across a treasure trove of vitality and I had a veracious appetite to push my body in search of physical pleasure. Being into such chemicals held a certain romantic air to it. I felt like the cool cat on the block, make no mistakes about it. "Swagger" or so I thought all those years back and it is rather easy to excite people at that age with acts of a daring nature.

I graduated school successfully securing me a place on a two year health and social care course and once I graduated, I went on to study nursing sciences for three years at the University of Nottingham, I drank heavily throughout my time at college and university – eight cans of European larger or a cheap pack of Strongbow cider would be a nightly routine quiet often with friends but nevertheless I would drink booze at home with my partner who was able to get served booze for my consumption. She is a little older. I was fifteen at the time. I am now thirty. She is still my sweetheart today, my fiancé except now she supports my sobriety as opposed to enabling my unhealthy obsession with booze and drugs.

At university, when I was coming of age the drink kept on pouring down my gullet, hammering those internal organs to the very edge of failure in addition to my daily ketamine habit. I couldn't string a sentence together at the best of times. I would stammer and splutter, murmurs to my friends and family. I was all too aware of my incapacities but through the desirable anesthetising nature of the ketamine, I did not seem to care much. I would snort at least a gram of crystallised "Ket" daily at the very least. The trips I had were stories for another time but I will say this; ketamine introduced me to alternative worlds that are visually comparable to films such as BladeRunner where no signs of one's surroundings could be perceived as actual reality. Ketamine causes complete traversal of an entire alternative plane of existence and completely dissolves the world around you when enough is snorted. I chased that sort of experience. The drunken state ketamine gave when small doses were administered were fun, no doubt about it but the real potential was only accessed when a trip ensued – the "K-Hole" and what a force of nature that stuff was in its peek popularity. God knows why. Conversation was reduced to just noise.

Once I got access to pharmaceuticals and narcotics such as morphine, benzodiazepines and especially heroin, they turned me on in life changing ways. I found a way to feel euphoria most of the time. I never actually found the kick I was looking for before dope despite extensive traversal on ketamine. Of course, I had sniffed cocaine out the naked bum crack of my fiancé, snorted methyl ephedrine by the grams, bombed amphetamines and MDMA until I was in love with the world and dancing with it in unison. I bedded more than a few women, each only for kicks. It was a seemingly ideal remedy for my restlessness but not so permanent nor sustainable. I recognised that. I was blowing off some steam and I had excess steam. I tried to be gay one night while out in town, passionately kissing a rather good-looking man in the middle of a bar. He was much older too. I was not supposed to even be in the joint, I was underage. He messaged me the next day but unfortunately for him – and me I guess; I am straight without no doubt. With the exception of falling in love and one does not profess to do that every day, and I do mean true love, it is extremely difficult to calm the tension, rest the hyperactivity without the use of drugs or drink in my case anyhow. In my instance, heroin and diazepam were the perfect cocktail and it truly was but they had another side to their bliss. I always found it curiously fantastic that these substances had no comedown it seemed. Although, if I would have known way back then, what I know now – I would have realised I gave no time for me to come down. I narrowly escaped death a few times on my road through my habit. It seemed sure worth it at the time and so you rinse and repeat not just through necessity but the sheer pleasure of that junk, that anesthetisation, oh so perfect, wholesome and complete. God, it's like warm syrup bringing to life a cooling body petrifying and decaying through lack of hard narcotics. So, the following piece is my account, story and shame.

*(Note, "Methadrone" is the synthetic reproduction and intensification of the Alkaloid Cathinone found in the Khat plant native to north-west Africa)

Chapter 3
"The Hit in the Nose and a Look of Junk"

"This is not creative writing but creative reading"
– William S Boroughs

Back in the toilet stalls in a bodega central to Nottingham City, I had snorted the two brown lines of heroin. I turn around and I was sitting on a filthy piss marinated toilet seat without care for my new Levi slacks I had not long since brought for more than a moderate price. Regarding the pants, my thought at that moment was, *Why didn't I spend the cash on this oh so perfect drug?* After all, you do not require expensive jeans to feel cool and dope will do that for you. Not the best look though I suppose. Stiff clothes from dirt, lack of bathing and withdrawal from the "opposing" square society does not make a fantastic look nor encourages one to prosper whatever that might mean. Regardless, I begin to feel warmth magically radiating throughout my perfectly relaxed body. I lose sight rapidly of my regrets and prosperities.

I have been told repeatedly by characters in the junk scene that snorting heroin is unheard of nowadays and it's a big waste of cash and dope, according to the needle freaks;

'Man, what you done with your food, dude? You dropped it!'

'Snorted it.'

I retort already on the verge of a nod. That's because snorting is my dig. The least I can avoid ravaging my physique with needle marks once I've rotated the puncture area several times forcing me into re-hitting veins to fucking destruction. Then again, I must keep an open mind. I didn't think of the psyche, more so my behaviour prior to presenting my hate on needles after all. It brings plenty of relief to the mind indeed but I truly believe that all pleasure is relief. This is an idea supported by academics such as William H Boroughs and a bipartisan of a majority of square doctors better versed on the subject in the first instance. Heroin will soothe if taken by the most route of ingestion, bar the stomach of which for some strange reason has significantly reduced affects speaking of course from experience.

Snorting does the trick perfectly; one of the closest access areas to spike the brain after all. And of course, it is more convenient for all the functional addicts too; working as lawyers, police agents, doctors etcetera, no track marks or funny chemicals cooking up aromas in the works lavatory.

I once worked with a junky physician who would self-administer morphine diverted from the hospital's surplus supply. It was destined for incineration after all. Similarly, I know a couple of queer nurses working in the critical care unit who would steal ketamine, Clonazepam and Pre-Gabalin. All to make sure they had something to look forward to at the end of their thirteen-hour long shifts. In that respect, having a locker full of stolen narcotics would make those drug fiends work faster and to a better level of efficiency. It's always best to have something to look forward to after all. I quite understand their actions. I would questionably obtain Valium and best of all (or in fact not) Oxycontin. Others are driven by cash and the prospect of taking a cruise around the Mediterranean. Us junky dig nodding off, taking trips back into our mother's womb, warm and in the arms of my fiancé. It is worth noting my better half would be sober.

Before I moved to Nottingham, I would commute by train from the polluted city full of interesting people, dangerous people and floaters from all walks of life, back home each evening to the deep suburbs where there were farms and fields and a beautiful family home. It is a large house and in a small village. It was however, out of the way from any signs of normality or I suppose the craziness you see in the cities. It left you wanting more. Well, it did me anyway. I liked the crazy city. What young person doesn't, I wonder? It's rather a paradox but cities are where the drugs are purer and plentiful and the parties are every night. No bi-weekly droughts because some suburban child dealer hasn't made his pick-ups. "Anyone for two for one bottles of Amyl Nitrate, a twenty deck of counterfeit cigarettes and knock off, diluted vodka guaranteed to accelerate mouth and throat cancer?" Seemingly this is some local's idea of a good Friday evening at the local. Soap Bar is also on the menu – the worst grade of hashish one might ever smoke. Not for me and I'm far from the upper class.

'What a ball ache commuting each day.'

My friends commented and I would have agreed if it wasn't for me anticipating an orgasmic ride home. Allow me to expand. There was no spunk involved, just opioids clinging to every receptor causing me to melt perfectly into the seat on the train home. I was in sheer pleasure, ecstatic yet calm and content on each train ride home. I looked forward to the commute as the thirteen-hour long shifts turns into powder of eighty milligrams of fast acting Oxycontin. What a beautifully elegant posture I would assume while turning the capsule of hard narcotics into snort worthy powder. I would snort the prolonged release Oxys by scrapping off the coating of the tablet thus to leave one with pure, unadulterated, immediately released Oxycontin. My goodness I had never been so fortunate to be in a public toilet in all my life. I'd bag up multiple tablets diverted from somewhere and sold on to me for cheap (back when sense of worth prevailed), scrap the coating off them to leave a naked white tab then I would crush them good then bag the powdered gold. This would be my caffeine equivalent while working one of the largest and busiest hospitals in the UK. I had no tolerance to drugs bar ketamine to speak of at this time but plenty and plenty of naivety and an unquenchable taste for booze and hard narcotics though still not habitual usage, physically anyway.

I once knew the daily affairs of a rather square appearing high school teacher. I did not stalk the man; only you get to know what's on each other's washing line when you cross paths, a large percentage of the time especially if your dealer is running late and you can bet, he is. I waited with this rather large guy, nicely tapered beard and a face red with acne. This encounter was around the time my habit on heroin was rather humungous and consisted of me needing speedballs at least four days a week; heroin and cocaine, sometimes crack, cocaine which the latter I regarded as a waste when some quality sniff was about. No pub dust for me. I would snort fish scale quality, uncut raw cocaine with my dope. The shots were wonderful. Absolute visceral and a psychical pleasure, it was complete speed and power. Reluctantly aware that such unearthly pleasures will not be achieved in normality. Unfortunately, even at a tender age, I knew all too much that such heights, happiness and contentment can only be achieved by some outside force. Drugs are a force to reckon with, that is for sure. Love is another great example of an entity powerful enough to shatter a heart, make one's turn to mush with empathy and of course ache for those around you less fortunate. Love is a strong substance. Love is the drug.

So, I met this school teacher a few times when picking up junk on my extended honeymoon with heroin. I was in the car chatting with my unlicensed pharmacist called Sam when Tomas, the teacher of maths, swung gleefully into the back of the jeep causing an impromptu suspension check.

'Hello, good to see you, Sam.'

He goes full of beans.

'You having the usual, **my** mate?' said Sam.

The "my mate" was emphasised, Tomas the teacher said, 'Yes of course and another half gram of brown on top.'

He speaks rather cautiously.

'Just this one time, mind you, Sam.'

He had addressed Sam in some attempt with real intention and then paused deep in thought. He was justifying his need for more H to his dealer for Christ's sake.

'Hey, Sam, this gear not up to much, Tomas complains.'

His eyes were pin pricked and glazed over. He was clearly fixed on dope and had a yen for more. It's never enough nor is it as powerful as one would like it to be.

Sam spoke softly but with matter of fact.

'Well, Jane and her fella both went over on two points, I served them last Tuesday and they are fucking fiend's man, so your tolerance is creeping up! That's your explanation right there!'

Sam asserted.

'Wonder if they pulled through?'

Sam looked at me doubtfully. He said he had had no orders from them since they overdosed. The prognosis looks nasty. I interjected.

'The smack's powdered gold, mate. Take it from me,' I said.

Tomas looked at me with a face of puzzlement. I could see the lights flick on bright in Sam's eyes. It would mean that Tom the teacher would be seeing a lot more of Sam and his cling film wraps of junk and it will only get more expensive once the rocks are rolling. It seems that a habit has a tight hold on Tomas already. That tolerance doesn't stay low for long there my friend,' I said. He is suffering from the blues but wacked out his mind on heroin. It won't be long now before Tomas the teacher shoots a little over his usual between his classes because he predicts a difficult next lecture. Rude students engrossed in their mobile phones – a pet hate of Tom's despite his level of intoxication. He is smacked up and to be frank, he couldn't care less now. He cares little about anything anymore.

Tomas the teacher had three options now. The self-administered Diamorphine had opened up a few doors. Before so, his options were limited. Now he could at least pursue one of three scenarios – pretty much all he could conjure in his drugged state of mind; hand out Valium spiked cups of Monster energy drink to his students (a staple drink the students dig for it's over the top caffeine content and of course excessive sugar). Kids start early nowadays. Blackened lungs, stuck together like outdated, black mozzarella cheese-like tar but with several hundred carcinogenetic chemicals in the place of calories. Young teen's lungs comparable with a 60-year-old miner who suffers with chronic, obstructive pulmonary disease is not a stretch of the imagination whatsoever. Teeth chock full of ugly metallic fillings, some missing and some rotting from the onset of gum disease caused by the amount of sugar they cannot get enough of and the bootleg cigarettes sold by all and sundry; pub goers, neighbours and connivance stores sold under the nose of the law, under the counter of course.

I digress slightly. So, to cause the class to kip through this two-hour lecture Tomas possibly could then catch a nod himself.

'Hell, I could certainly fix up without a doubt.'

He can set his alarm on his Apple phone to wake him. He has a baggie full of cheap Valium in his desk, pressed pills of course. Don't go wasting the real McCoy's diazepam in the blisters, however the presses are effective nonetheless even with the potential to poison with a large dose of fentanyl at worst, knock them out for a couple hours at best. Tomas the teacher will just have to give the curriculum work to his students to do at home. A little homework never hurt after all. That's one radical idea, he drifts off into a day dream. He could overdose, get a shot of Narcan while pulled away by paramedics, off to the hospital, CT scan to check levels of brain damage from when he stopped breathing, jobs in tatters, and his partner in hysterics. Preferably not. Or he could fix sensibly and continue his performance and see how long he can maintain? Going home to nod is not an option for Tomas. Phantom study days can only be used once in a while not each week. He knows this very job is his lifeline in more ways than one. *I need my brown head master,* he imagines pleading like one of his students to go home because he is sick. A pleading junky trying half arse excuses to keep his folk medicine coming and avoid the sickness that looms over his head every day is essential. At night after work, he fixes his shot and he sleeps like a baby – out like a light, fresh for tomorrow. And the cycle continues. It's his 'night cap', if you please. A pleading, begging junky is a disgusting sight especially in occupations such as teaching and nursing but all junkies know the score until they score or don't.

I felt a fear and something else rather sinister for the teacher at the time. Not of his demise. I suppose it was some clarification I am not the only fool to dig smack but I guess I should know that already. The dude looked typically like a teacher, young, smart, handsome, lady friend called Louise he was saying, a smart wrist watch and a good honourable career. Bank account certainly appeared healthier before this little daily routine of drug use began. His lady friend will be aware more than likely and perhaps on the horse herself, why she turned him on to it. He always scored for £50 of each meaning, 50 squid for the wonderful brown and 50 crisp ones for the crack cocaine. Nice order by all accounts, but that's a considerable quantity of drugs for personal use. You wonder if he shares them. Not before shaving a hit off each rock, first he will not. Poor partner sat at home sick and yenning for the drugs he is holding. Goodness knows what his work performance is like at the school. Excellent I suspect, for a time anyhow. I can empathise I lot more with that. That's a story best saved for later. Fixing is the priority, fixing will always be priority for a heroin fiend. Fixing is needed to remain human at that moment in order to deal with whatever life throws at you. Better it be hard narcotics than a divorcé, job loss and mental breakdown after all.

In any instance sniffing the gear up the nose fixes you nicely. It's a quick ritual that if adequately prepared for is rather indulgent or on the flip side a quick hit that can be done off a toilet seat if caught in a hurry. I even found it to be a pleasurable ritual of preparation that I believed was a fitting preface to the forthcoming warmth and calm. The heroin was blessed to provide. It's no fucking use a powder; it needs to be in our body saturating the cells. In fact, I believe the acts of which I am practicing has been found to be a ritual long performed by our ancestors. Maybe the Greek god Dionysus, in all his ancestral might, the son of Zeus after all, introduced the practice of snorting plant medicines up the nose to achieve higher states are seemingly much similar to his celebration and encouragement of using grape to produce alcoholic wine. Which grew exponentially of course and I thank Dionysus, he did. As it so happens these words are written, these ideas captured and these observations documented are by the hands of a man drunk and sedated. The beavers of brown at lunch get their raising blood pressure down so to resume work calmly and collected like. Some of heroin's redeeming qualities – I give thought for the teacher. Hindsight I should have thought more about my own life but all's dandy at the time. The comparison is frighteningly similar.

The initial reason I dug into snorting the shit is because you get the entire amount of product in your body and there is no wastage, not a grain gone, caught in a wisp of smoke travelling out the crack in the window. It's a decent way of testing your score too. If you've been fucked over you will smell the powdered make-up foundation, they use to cut the heroin. Milk sugar is a common and better bash for brown if ultimately required. In actual fact I told my regular retailer of my dope that because of the route I take, I taste and moreover consume the adulterants as if they were all active substances (when pinning or injecting a junk hog tends to boil away the crap using their works predominantly consisting of his silver, blackened spoon and a used fag butt as his filter. He drops the yellow stained filter in to the spoon and the liquidities of his heroin is now in his warped mind ready for injection) which was disconcerting and a bring down at the time when I should be nodding. I exaggerated of course; his gear is always of good potency. Complaining about one's heroin once obtained can be a challenge. I live by the rule a good friend once disseminated to me in relation to the topic of buying drugs. "Do not bite the hand that feeds you". Very true especially if one is an addict to the food being peddled. Complaining must be done stoned, on Valium however, it is very rare a dealer will cut you off entirely as long as you have cash and haven't been strongly alarmed by any law enforcement. I forgot the shit was actually illegal. Same with most drugs mind.

So however due to my daily order of the dark stuff which was beginning to cost upwards of fifty pounds per day on top of buying cocaine, Valium and some psychedelics when they came along for kicks on a rainy day, I felt at liberty to mention the adulterant issues with my supplier. I wasn't a particular fan of the perfume used in the product as it was. I enjoyed the vinegar smell and taste as it drips down the gullet. His reaction was surprising and from that day forth I got nice large rocks of heroin, still adulterated for sure but its rock form provided me a sense of security. His reason for fulfilling my extraordinary request to alter his business practice and to stop cutting his gear came most likely from the amount of cash I was peeling off to him making my request all but a very minor loss on his behalf. The dirty excitable ritual of shaving my heroin rocks onto a sheet of paper resulting in a powdered form is my preferred method of use. However, such methods are rarely accessible in boozer lavatories. They just don't accommodate for the junky. Its bad business practice on their part if you ask me. They take the coke user into consideration after all. My mind turns back to me having strange, distasteful thoughts. I hesitated though again and thought about what all those slick old heroin cats had said to me when scoring, "Pin the gear man. I'm saving you money by suggesting it. The hits better too." This interested me some but I never yet gave in to any temptations and believe me there were plenty of temptations all the time.

Every day main lining the dope went through my mind. The days working as a nurse, skin popping morphine to replace a strange and incurable sense of loss or a piece missing inside which I couldn't really put my finger on. All I know for sure is that it hurt like someone had burnt a cigarette hole deep in my heart, full of ash and carcinogens. It was all too often that I would think about that void and how to best fill it. Drugs were the easy way to cool the burn. Call me an optimistic pessimist. My two cents in life is full of monumental highs and soul crushing blues. If a person argues they have never felt the blues, then they simply need to keep on living. I have gone to realise however that it is not necessarily too important whether you feel up or down on a particular day, it's what you do with the energy that makes the difference. A perfect example of this art form is expression through music from the blues sang and played since the '50s to the happy house music of the '90s. And everything in between that turns you on. It's a paradox that can on the one hand destroy a character and on the other strengthen the soul and subsequently one's resolve.

So, I was not turned on by injecting my hit, pinning they call it, although a menacing curiosity niggled at me without fail during snorting the dope and it was especially exacerbated when options for pinning were plentiful. Pharmacies tend to offer clean works to junkies and steroid freaks in the interest of public health. Certainly, a good call on the government's part, especially if one regards the characters in the circles, I tended to move in. Being around junkies shooting their brown beauty on coaches around me increases the exposure levels to altered states of being. For example; I doubt that it is a fable that injecting heroin feels like sex with God himself. Intravenous drug use is risky business though. "Is that feeling of warmth pulsing through your every fibre worth a pound of flesh"? Could be I summarised this in my head with haste. Skin popping is as far as I took this horrific, obsessive compulsion and I thank my lucky stars that it remained this way.

Chapter 4
Back in the Old Toad Boozer

When snorted the heroin is a pleasant scent of sweet vinegar which when read by a non-user sounds repulsive. But to a junky it is not. As the powder travels up the nose, a junky can almost smell the opium plant of which it once came.

Once the junk is snorted, the first symptom to be relieved is the dryness of the mouth and throat and the general feeling of sickness is cured. A sense of triumph is felt. My muscles that were weak and aching all melted away and radiated with warmth and strength. My bowel content seemed to firm up immediately and my digestive system began to muse. I felt hungry, even thirsty for a Guinness. The pain and in turmoil I had felt in my stomach was replaced by a warm euphoria. I had energy but was calm and content, anxiety eradicated. I rubbed my eyes which were no longer sore nor dilated. I looked around but this time paying attention to my surroundings, on arrival I was too fixated on the junk to care to look. I could have been in a church, shop or cruise ship. I just required the use of their facilities so to get well, straighten out, sharpen up and of course, get high.

I exited the stall nodding to greet the old men still chatting about their planned vacation as I left the toilet. I was in a traditional English pub complete with a collection of beer mats hung on display, gold polished beer pumps and a long varnished wooden bar. I stand out too much with my ginger hair for me to leave the place without buying anything so I order a Guinness. Guinness is a good choice when on opioids as it seems to settle well in the stomach. Most other booze curdles causes sickness and is rather unenjoyable.

As I take the pint and sit down, I tell myself that the drink I had brought is certainly justified, after all I did use their facilities for my sordid and illegal drug consumption. *Best to buy a pint in the interest of good karma*, I thought. Although, I am in a rough part of the city and I suspect that their lavatory has been used by numerous drug users over the years. Nevertheless, I do try to keep some of my morals. I sit down in a notably empty pub, the air thick with stale cigarette smoke permeating from the wallpaper which is like a blotter paper containing nicotine. Even the fucking paint is impregnated with tobacco. I am sitting in an ash tray no less. A slight realisation of the circumstances in which I find myself, flows inconsequently through my sedated mind. It makes my stomach churn just thinking about what I did to myself, how disgraceful to all my friends, family and fiancé I was but such is the nature of the drugs which sedate such rationalisation.

While sitting there high and pondering, it wasn't long before an elderly man who looked like a victim of the crack epidemic sat down next to me and asked me openly with matter-of-fact weather I would like to buy any Viagra or ten milligram diazepam pills. My ears pricked up of the sound of the latter. I said to forget the Viagra. 'I don't need that (since my cock is too limp from drug intoxication, no lush worker nor pill would be of much assistance I imagine, sexual desire is replaced by the junk).'

'But how much are the Valium?'

'They're a pound a piece no matter how many you buy.' He warned me.

I said, 'I'll take a strip of twenty.'

So, we squared up, and I ordered another Guinness maybe to celebrate the score.

Diazepam and booze are a sure kick and when combined with junk it will make a man feel invincible. I chucked five of the blue pills down my neck and gulped a swag of ale. The trouble is now a man on such a cocktail of substances tends to make ill thought-out decisions. It wasn't long until I was revisiting the stalls to sniff more dope and this time, the lines I cut were considerably larger in size.

I drank three more pints of draft Guinness and I felt the glow of the alcohol. The five diazepam pills began to take effect which made me confidently dopey and happy. All in all, a pleasant feeling. The heroin caused me to nod there in the pub, sitting with an empty glass and my head nearly falling into my lap. I know from experience that this combination of drugs kills a large amount of its users but that itch to get out the wrap of junk and sniff it until I glow warmer and rush with untold pleasures and relief is completely unfathomable and powerful. "But this is how folk die", rang a voice in my head… my hand subconsciously placed upon my wallet in my pocket in which contained the small wrap of the remaining junk.

I read a study at university where rats will choose a particular drug to consume as an alternative to food when given the chance and they will continue this behaviour until they perish. The drugs are usually cocaine or heroin. I sit there in that bar thinking of the crude similarities between a rat and a man, more accurately, the rat's resemblance to a dope fiend. The thought is bitter and depressing. *Maybe another Valium or some more gear is in order to quell such disgusting thoughts?* I think to myself on guard and ready to take action.

As I sit in my drug induced stupor, I notice that the elderly man ravaged by years of crack smoking was supping up and leaving the bar. The diazepam he had sold me was exceptional. My heroin kick potentiated by its presence. A sudden panic shot through me like a lost child might experience in a shopping mall when he loses sight of his mother. I staggered to follow him out.

'What about a phone number so I can get hold of you should I need more of the stuff you sold me earlier?' I asked with a drawl.

His thin slackened face turned to greet me and he huffed a breath of annoyance through the few yellow teeth that remained.

'There is no number!'

He barked.

'But I drink in here most days so meet me here if you want more.'

He ordered.

'I have boxes of thousands at home but they'll go quick.'

He warned with matter of fact.

'Meet me same time tomorrow.'

He suggested this. I agreed I would, almost an automatic answer, I will have to plan picking up my heroin around meeting him. I ought not to disregard the fact my fiancé will be off work and so would be expecting some time with me also. Being a junky is a full-time trade.

It seems that psychic and emotional defence is a priority around this neighbourhood for sure, though I doubt the disease is contained here. Iggy Pop was kind of right.

'You wan anuva strip lad?' the old guy asked through his crack infested throat – damaged and torn from years of cigarettes and drug usage. Of course I wanted another strip and he knew so too. I could detect it in his attitude.

Mental arithmetic has always been a subject of contempt for me. I am neither motivated to improve nor well versed in the first instance, however I quickly evaluate the balance of my overdraft in my head and I calculate how many of the diazepam on offer I can afford without losing my travel fare home or leaving me short of cash for the next couple of weeks living. I still work see, unlike a lot of full-time junkies but I need junk to keep up the work and to feed my dependant hunk of flesh like a robot requiring computing or a Ford Fiesta oiling. I need junk in order to rise out of bed in a morning; to warm up and have energy – energy to obtain more heroin, to uphold my manor and get by in my day-to-day activities. It seems that I must have a substance in my system in order to muster vitality and escape from my larger appetite for the other various drugs I dig. Junk tends to do this; I find with a few exceptions. There are always exceptions; cocaine and benzodiazepines namely. If my opioid receptors are saturated with junk however, all other drugs are but a bonus – not essentials.

My relationship with narcotics extends somewhat into an obsession, certainly addiction which subsequently leads to whole alternative perspective on life, the need and the yen to learn more while of course having as much fun as possible. After all, what raging pig bastard has the fucking energy to waste the time of their life without the prospect of true unadulterated fun and debauchery? I know some folks that are sure enough. Guess they will and maybe have had the last laugh after all.

My obsession with substances and altering my consciousness began when I was young. Booze was plentiful and the food rich, the company at the table warm and wonderful. These gatherings of our family were held at my mamma and granddad's sweet old cottage. I still remember the smell of old stone walling and cork. The garden was rich of flowers and that gave off beautiful scents of perfumes. Memories of a queen bee collecting its honey; a red robin visiting my mamma's bird bath for a wash, logs burning in the open fire place, warming the hearth. I had great love and respect for my mama and she would look after me when I was young while my mother and father worked hard.

I have beautiful memories of these times when I must have been four or five years of age. I always thought my memory to be accurate and good. I remember doing art work with my mama. We would make characters out of wooden cloth pegs called "peg people". I believe my sister kept one for sentimental purpose. We would make cards on special days or to show my affection for my mother when she came home from work to pick me up to take me back home. We would often greet her with home baked cakes too. I never recall a moment of unhappiness or grief while with my mamma. Her empathetic nature would allow me to experiment with what I liked. I considered this a quality much to my father's dismay. Authority however breeds rebellion at the first opportunity and so, my problems with authority began. I remember fearing authority at first, most probably due to physical punishment received from my dad. He had an alternative way of keeping people in order. It never worked for me. Despite differences I love my father very much. We're more similar than each of us dare to admit.

I once got a kick – maybe my first ever visceral kick, from seeing Michael Jackson perform live on the TV on a show called 'Top of the Pops' and so after my discovery I would imitate his singing and dancing. I was attracted by the way he moved, defying the laws of physics with fluidity and it was seemingly effortless. My mama would indulge me. My attempts of imitating him were obviously crude but I got a kick from my mama tying a white tea towel around my waist modelling his outfit in the music video of "How You Make Me Feel". I was also turned on to The M people – a hit band who gained much deserved success in the nineties. Heather Small on the vocals gave me the goose bumps coursed by pleasure that creeped up my spine, sometimes overwhelming my cheeks and face. I fell in love with music and more so, the way it made me feel. I could not get enough. My mum would pick me up and we would listen to Michael Jackson repeatedly on cassette on our journey home in rush hour traffic. I vividly remember the glow of the warmth I felt when listening. Me and my mum share the same love for music to this very day.

Chapter 5
Chipping

When a man begins experimentation with narcotics of the opioid variety, he will most likely claim to use only at the week's end – a "chipper" as they call them (those who claim to consume the substance casually). Note chippers rarely stay so for long. It is more accurate to state that "chipping" is a beginning of an addiction. Often the user will then deem the substance useful to utilise day to day to help him get by "more smoothly". The feelings the junk causes; warmth, reassurance and consolation that he is successful in his every endeavour. Although often the drug administered is regarded as insignificant to his favourable performance. This illusion is often the point where the junk takes hold and the person uses his chosen elixir to "aid" him in his future conquests. After all he believes he has found a hack of sorts, 'thee' hack. Very soon his tolerance to the drug will increase with incredible and unbelievable velocity. He will most often disbelieve in this phenomenon at first however the moment he wakes up one morning sneezing in rapid successions, profusely sweating, his restless legs squirming akin to volatile snakes under duress all the while experiencing a feeling of developing decay gradually ravaging his body and mind. Only then does he somehow begin to believe in the power of the drug in which a vast majority of men have been unable to tame never mind barely survive. "This shit feels too nice". Like a full body orgasm, only a pill, powder and puncture mark away. Fuck yes! I remember evaluating. Why not? Does that not sound good? The problem now is the user starts work at 9am and his retailer of his precious junk is running late. They nearly always are running late. The restless addict phones in work while he paces the kitchen.

'Hi, can I speak to the manager please?' he asked breathless. Anxious and needing a shit, "speaking" sings the voice down the phone, you say with all the politeness you can apply.

'I'm running late, some drunk held up the tram.'

'Be here as soon as possible please.'

The manager directs with obvious annoyance.

The dealer turns up half hour later and you score. The excitement, the energy! You run to his jeep, jump in and do the deal. Why, he has crack too. Why not? I am late anyway. I'd turn in to work an hour later, eyes dilated, full of chemical induced energy and ready to go, throat red raw from the crack, voice all hoarse.

This was a typical circumstance for me to find myself in. My stomach seemed to rot from the inside out, state of wellness-euphoria more accurately displaced violently by sickness that only worsens until the will to stay clean dissolves. A matter of only four hours sometimes for me I'm embarrassed to admit. And the cash I have spent! "Oh the amount is sickening". Fifty pounds for a stone of H no larger than a marble no less. Oh, but that kick… that kick is too much to manage by any conceivable method compatible with sustained healthy living, financially, socially and biologically. This has been argued by many of academic junkies over the years with a few claiming the use of opioids and other such narcotics are not injurious to health. I can only profess to agree with this concept to a certain degree. For one, it depends dramatically on the quality and purity of the substance used. Although, the theory of minimal damage to health from drug experimentation only extends to "drug use" not "drug abuse". The line becomes blurred more often than none. Ten milligrams of diazepam is enough, what the hell, five milligrams would do! But this is not how it plays out. My experience with drug use versus abuse and good intensions went often something like follows; I take my morning fix of heroin – around hundred milligrams. Then the "heroism" takes effect and one is strong armed by Mr Brown to potentiate the buzz with a benzodiazepine. Ten milligrams of diazepam "I'll be good and precautious" I kid my pathetic self. An over dose easily will stop a man from breathing and my better half is at work. The thought of her finding my body lifeless and blue churns my stomach so much; I visit the toilet to relieve my loose bowel. Not out of concerns for my own welfare I might add but the distress and heartache I'd most likely course my fiancé and family. Anger I would imagine too, reaction to my selfish endeavours. I am alone with my demons. "DANGER DANGER". A distant voice rings out a warning in my head. I chew a ten milligram more of Valium to quell my anxiety. Chewing it will get it in to my blood stream quicker. Haste is preferable. Why wait? Would you?

I stagger to a source of booze and know that from past kicks, chugging a beer will be certain to suppress that nervous system that little bit further while my pleasure receptors muse and I morph into a lump of human pleasure. I might even achieve a nod. Dangerous! But I have survived it before and in no time at all floods of confidence having me lining up another line of brown powder and "one last benzo", I emphasis the quotation marks. This scenario unfolded like this for me most days for three years more or less. One would think one would learn, wouldn't you? Wouldn't you? No, you would not. Muscle, physical strength and even mental stability are rarely enough to keep the ball from rolling once it starts its descent in to a hellish cycle of madness. Then comes cocaine but I digress slightly too fast. Adding the cocaine to the concoction came about a bit later, when I began chasing higher levels of consciousness, often unconsciousness. My progressive use of cocaine started later and is recited in the continuation of my tale.

When one gets a habit, they are introduced to a sect made up entirely of bums, addicts, hipsters, dealers, drop-outs (Faithfull's of Timothy Leary in a diluted, unaware manor) – William Boroughs once lectured on the subject of "what we know and what we do not know we know". The brain is also a filter theorised by some. It prevents us from becoming overwhelmed by the vast amount of information we actually know however not so much use. Does this mean then those drugs are an amulet to buff the filter system? For instance, Cannabis Sativa and LSD dissolves the filter while smack, booze and benzodiazepines filter more so. Cocaine lies somewhere in the middle as might amphetamines only the latter two work more predominantly on the ego and it's enhancement. Maybe when we use these drugs or tools in some respects, it enables us to really put those rose-coloured glasses on something uglier and depressing? I personally think so. Through the years I've taken many drugs, tuned into the experience the tools gave me, and allowed myself to demolish an ego that is so Viking in sects such as the gym-nut or the steroid freaks. So that's great! But now how do you know when to stop and if so, can you? Before long you're going to render yourself vulnerable. You begin to crave that gym after all.

There is bad luck in attracting fools of which some may argue, I myself belong and professionals living an alternative life when not self-administrating rectal suppositories of Valium on late morning breakfast breaks at the local city hospitals, a subject in which I am knowledgeable from matter of experience.

There exists a large community of sex workers too, an age-old profession. A lucrative market if you have the looks. Especially suitable line of work if one smokes crack alongside maintaining a junk habit. None of the aforementioned sectors of the "drug" community are, as individuals, inherently bad people. They are twisted by a force of nature only the person themselves can explore and is not for someone else to truly diagnose although it is quite obvious drug addiction plays a pivotal role. Eventually the working man will be out of work simply because his supply of medicine has not arrived on time. But I digress again, symptoms of drug use for sure – back now to my story.

Chapter 6
"Just the One"

The three pints of Guinness has taken a proportion of the money I need to acquire more drugs and so maintain the subsidies of the narcotic enterprise. I hesitate at the ghost offering me the commodities and ask him to accompany me to a cash point with a view to conduct further business. I am certain that the balances will not compute and the sale and subsequent receipt of the extra diazepam is all but a fantasy stemming from the viscera and encouraged by what feels like a weighty great ape riding my back attempting to feed my addiction but lacking in rational thought. Is this exercise then pointless and rejection of the offer imminent? Absolutely not speaks out the junky in me, opportunities are around most corners although is luck really on my side? A faint hope that my bank balance has somehow reimbursed itself is obviously a symptom of the drug addict. Stalling I suppose, but business transactions come in many forms especially outside of the walls of the Queen's banks.

One can always spot an old time junky. Their body is thin, statue small and their hygiene unspoken for. They wear stiff cloths only for the primal reason to wear them – warmth and to keep dry, if they are lucky; they afford a level of comfort.

The smell they permeate is mixture of stagnant sweat main contents of which will be drugs, clothing soaked heavy in thick poisonous counterfeit cigarette smoke, dark ales and a fleeting scent of undiagnosed disease. A master in the trade often will don a limp when compared to a pirate however acquired, through multiple abscesses and other injection injuries sustained over years of slamming drugs into their once perfect veins. But the most recognisable trait, noticeable amongst all others is their ability to almost jog to their next destination, this is in order to play out their next trick move to obtaining more junk and or crack to fix them back to human from sick lobotomised absentee. The prospect of picking up more drugs causes a storm of intense emotions; excitement, anxiety and relief. When I score, the act is exactly that, a score-point up. Functionality is only a short snort, shoot, or plug away from realisation and it is a certain.

I struggle to keep up with the man I now know as "Cabin". I have not asked yet of the origin of his name. He navigates his way almost gracefully and with haste to the nearest automated teller. I stagger behind perilously trying to avoid falling flat on my face as the Guinness soaks slowly through my violated organs progressively intoxicating my mind, dissolving more of the Valium while dangerously suppressing my central nervous system as this all amalgamates with the junk. "The brain is a selfish organ!" a drug worker once enthusiastically proclaimed. I never gave it much thought until now. *This is my final day of kicks;* I verbalise to myself to somehow set it in stone driven by optimism – note "heroin" a play of the word "heroic" to best describe the feeling it gives the user. I agree on its accuracy that's for sure.

As I staggered behind him closely but not too close that I might be regarded as his associate by the general public as a sliver of ego shines through; I smile a coy smile believing I had found the ultimate fix and that my existence was somehow superior, like I'd discovered the secret elixir that will be the driving force for a better existence in life. Yet, I was trailing a man half decomposed by that very narcotic I claim aids my pursuits. Cabin rendered himself blind in one eye to get the fix his cells so desperately craved. He shot the dope straight into the capillaries in the eye. He had exhausted all other avenues. Even the veins on his cock were apparently out of action – "collapsed" he informed me nonchalantly through a bark. How narcotics are able to trick the user in to such fantasies of perfection is an extreme reaction to drug addiction. I was blind to it at the time, as blind as the man I followed; salivating for what seemed a pointless endeavour. Drugs are rarely free and if they are I would personally stay away. Hot shots still circulate the world of junk, catch one of those and your time is up, like an old school Mickey fin. Apparently, supremacist retailers of junk are combining the heroin with an unannounced dose of fentanyl or similar to whatever lethal chemicals can liquidate the populations of undesirables. The American populus are seeing this unfold on most streets in most states. The true root of all evil in the junk world. I heard the Pakistanis are perceived to course a level of threat by the local dope men. Why, I do not know or understand. Pakistan is a great source for poppy farming thus subsequent supply despite race of the retailer. I suppose any competition in the supply chain will inevitably piss off some retailer enough to start a street war. The brainless endeavour of a poisoned shot rarely fails to make an impact on the planned target and only kills a proportion of the pedlar's customers. With this in mind despite masqueraded by a mix of hard drugs, I still remember somehow that annoying this man is a bad call. Especially when doing business. I remember feeling apprehensive but I fail to be cautious and continue my plan at somehow playing him out of more pills. Cabin will not take it kindly; I remember deciding, his next fix of crack depends on me coming through good and his cells are most certainly hungry for chemical subsidence. I can sense them from one junky to another. There exists such a sense.

A fleeting realisation that I was cut from the exact same clothes as the guy I was trailing only my physique less ravaged yet drifted inconsequently through my mind. I look down at my bloated stomach to confirm my suspicion. A toxic mix of gas and fluid unable to digest churns and stagnates in the system. Perhaps permanent scaring? What an ugly thought however true.

We arrive at the cash machine, graffiti scrawled all over the buttons and I put on a pantomime of checking my balance and attempting to withdraw non-existent cash. "The bank has plenty of money"! I double damned the banking institution theatrically. Just enough for another couple of strips is all I ask! But no. The cash point will not pay out the forty pounds I need to score. Not today. I make this fact known to my associate, Cabin, by banging my fist hard on the cash point and cursing under my breath "fuck". I glanced despairingly at Cabin and a gruesome grin of satisfaction filled his face like he had been stimulated by some tender force; he had all the time he hoped for, building himself up too.

'Maybe there is another way we can do business, friend.'

He croaked noticing my predicament. His suggestion reeked of sexual propositions.

'No way, man.'

I object.

'Two strips of Valium are not worth the bother and emotional trauma that is bound to follow – no offence but I am straight, mister.'

I added believing this would nudge him into understanding.

'I agree,' Cabin replied to my protest. 'But I bet, and I am not usually a betting man, that judging by that sweat building on your brow right there.'

He pointed with a long soot-covered finger, revealing his hideous blue hands, tattooed with unrecognisable art work and sore, bulbous pin marks from all his recent intravenous drug use. His nails were black, the entry mark of his last fix of poison has leaked yellow puss that has crusted over like a rotten corn flake. He pointed with his finger, his uncut nail nearly touching my forehead, he continued.

'I bet that you'll be feeling junk sick soon. Am I right, lad?'

He spoke, cock sure of himself and indeed he was right. He could see it plain as day and a grin of satisfaction; almost excitement took over his filth covered face which gave way to a profile that suggested planning – scheming like something on his mind was pleasing him. He seemed to care little about my lack of funds.

I had dipped into my baggie of heroin back there in the pub which subsequently and rather unfortunately depleted my stash for the coming days. I could do with junk but then again, a junk hog can always do with junk. The shopping list of narcotics required has increased and anxiety about future sickness heightened accordingly. I cannot afford to be sick and nor have I the time to kick the habit just yet. A body dependant on a moderate amount of heroin will, in my experience, demand two weeks in order to overcome a majority of the symptoms of withdrawal and this sickness will, without a doubt, render the man bed bound for at least a quarter of that fortnight. Work or even recreational activity besides substance indulgence is out the question when kicking. One is physically unable to muster the energy to do anything but be ill and that is even before exploring the psychological horrors that loom ahead when that supply of brown rock to the body's cells is cut off. What a dilemma and with zero cash, the future appeared grey, hopeless and I'm beat.

'I can fix you up with a wrap of the brown stuff on top of those strips of Valium, hell, I'll even throw in a rock of the white and a few promethazine!'

I nearly thought out aloud "sure" and not giving two fucks either but I hesitated. I got a brief lash of excitement accompanied by dread and shame.

'I dig cocaine with such ferocity, I have sniffed it until I am teetering on the edge of psychosis, I have enjoyed it at civilised drinking gathering post meals and used it (or misused it) at a great number of parties in my younger days. It is still exhilarating and a most fun past time however extremely overpriced due to its associations with upper class junky's. This is a myth. Cocaine is not a substance reserved for the wealthy at all. Its universal use has made it common practice such like the sale of cannabis in places where sensible laws prevail such as Amsterdam.

'But this is crack which will do superbly... a speedball nonetheless! Nonetheless if taken with my junk.'

My internal monologue is now muted in an attempt to avoid too much indulgence. I am faced with a real dilemma, crack's nasty and I should split and score elsewhere else. But this idea is impossible, I need to score again. This might be my only chance to pick it up for this evening, I mean, it is getting on five o'clock now and it's dark and cold outside on the streets.

'For the items you wish to have of me, a young man like yourself could do an old gentleman a little favour? You young bucks love mixing your dark with that Promethazine, don't you?'

Not allowing me time to answer.

'I know a girl who guzzles that codeine cough syrup. You should meet her soon if we are going to come to an agreement.'

He dropped out losing his tether slightly, they call it "lean yanno"! Yank gear I believe. Mind, they have the taste for pharmaceuticals I am led to believe. The United States of America's universal anaesthetic is junk, methamphetamine and tobacco.

It's not a bad kick, he ponders, staring blankly into the distance with his only operating eye while the other moves seemingly without control and his jaw falls relaxed almost in ore from his thin spectral face.

'And what is the favour?' I asked, half knowing the answer but my curiosity, or more like, the possibility of scoring drove me to pursue the matter further.

'Well, I like to smoke rocks of crack cocaine and it gets my cock twitching and pulsating, the veins big enough to shoot smack into, my balls ache with the over production of semen and the only remedy is junk, which is preferable, a hooker, well, pounds are better spent or there is masturbation I suppose – but the latter is a ball ache man. No energy to tug. Wanking is a bum out on smack, that's for sure, man. I'm getting on forty, you know, kid.'

He spoke casually and almost comparable to a lecturer at university.

I say affirmatively that the Viagra he tried to flog me earlier should work magic on him then!

'It's not that getting a rise is the issue here, friend, it's my desire to fuck or be fucked. All men need loving,' he said almost in desperation. 'Even us beat up junk fiends.'

He assured me. But sexual contact? There is not much requirement for it. Gear sorts that out for us doesn't it, kid? A rhetorical question. I felt immediate discomfort that he had used the word "us". The ugly truth for one fleeting moment became painfully plain to see. We were similar and more so than I would care to admit aloud or to myself.

'If such a transaction was to be satisfied, I want a taste of the products you promise to pay me in return for my—' I hesitate, for the services. The thought of verbalising such hideous deals I am committing myself to is far too painful for words.

'My lady will sort you out a taste of them both on arrival at my house just down here. Come over, man!'

He encouraged.

'We will sort you out, my man, come on… my girl is very accepting of new faces and you seem like fresh meat, alright. Their ain't no better commodity out there.'

' She's a chipper,' He told me in a stupidly high-pitched voice. 'They call them chippers due to the tendency to only use junk in a controlled manner.' He informs me like I don't know shit. Like many can control their lust for alcohol by a glass of ale here and there, this is not possible with junk. Again, like I'm unaware.

'Your lady?' I say inquisitively.

He laughed a laugh that seemed to rip apart his lungs and larynx, he cackled, crocked and coughed at regular intervals until he finally spat the creation of phlegm, we all heard during its production. It shot from his mouth, a black and green mix of chemical impregnated snot and most probably the blood indicated steady erosion of his nasal cavities. He cursed his H retailer for cutting the shit with some bad "bash" (bash is street slang from powders used to cut the fine pure brown).

'No wonder what it does to my lungs putting that shit in a man's dope. Does he want one less customer?'

He barked almost having an asthma attack. He caught his breath and lit a fag.

'She's not my lady.'

He continues, 'She's the lady of the house. She's everyone's lady, looks after us all, whenever she is holding and someone is sick, she will set them up with a taste.'

People of such calibre are often looked upon admirably within the junk circle of people. Of course, they are, but only awaiting the next junky leaper to suck her tit.

Chapter 7
Talking About My Girl

Me and Cabin keep on walking down the back streets of nowhere. The darkness makes the trip even more dangerous and I can feel rays of apprehension fighting through my drug laced neurons. I fish for reassurance.

'So, I say, she won't mind me dropping by for that dope then, right?'

Trying to leave out the sexual payment part in some hope that he would forget. I know in my hearts of hearts he won't but maybe this lady of the house is a more decent dope fiend. I know even in a land of nods and dreams, that the shot that should be presented to me will certainly not come free. One can dream though, one can fantasise.

With such a barrier between me and said drugs, I am clinging to the plan with a steady grip – I should let go and get out of the situation but the possibility of scoring is too enticing. There is no getting off the ride while in motion as it goes on.

'Just quickly suck the tip end only; and I do emphasis only and then make them for all they have got and bounce double quick out of there.'

That's my plan set out by some internal monologue. Not much thought power contributing. It's Comforting to know that my internal abilities to think somewhat rationally at least has stayed with me for now and hasn't hazed up to the point where I would most definitely become absolutely fucking useless. Nothing short of a disgraced waste to those around me that matter, a cancer on society some may say. But it's not over to the fat lady sings goes the old saying which, in my current circumstances, the analogy may could well be fitting.

'So, are we on, young lad?'

There is no answer needed. He's already sussed out my plight and knows all too well I should be game. Cabin begins to dart-still limping but fast with me trailing behind, his stench absolutely noticeable yet indescribable except necroses comes to mind.

'My God, I ask myself, do I smell the same?'

It's only a matter of time. A bout of paranoia jolts my viscera and weighs heavy on my chest.

'I bath and at least keep up some sort of appearance but granted the junkies priorities slip once sister morphine arrives.'

'Fuck it!' I exclaim out loud so even my compadre can hear. 'This is my last one, my last shot and my last day in this paradoxical hellish dream. So, I better go out with a bang.' After all, I have weeks of hard labour to squirm out of this junk habit after today's last fix when the sun goes down and the moon lights the sky. I say again this time to myself, 'Just the one more.'

Cabin obviously heard my reckoning and replied in a long drawl, it's almost theatrical but no less a warning, 'Keep on telling yourself that, son, keep telling yourself that. I retorted argumentatively, this WILL be my last graceful shot of dope, I need it no more. It's time to clean up, baby. And indeed, it should be but will it be so? I don't really know. The highs, the kicks are immense no doubt however the lows are agonising pain mental and physical. I shall need to make a list of symptom managements because I sure can't go down the cold turkey route. I like the turkey warm.'

'Are we there yet, dude?' I ask cabin straight if a little too straight.

'Patience, boy, he demands, patience! You think a gal with her huge tits hanging out is going to appear like a gogo girl with your fix on a platter?'

'No, no you must wait boy we all have to wait.'

He rasps a voice of warning. He continues his limped march deeper down the street now.

'It's number 57', laddo You'll forget this place, mate, if you'd be so kind?'

Cabin politely warned. I retort with a yes. I can't see much course to revisit anyway; Cabin's change in demeanour certainly has perked up. Drugs are nearby. Here lies my final go around.

We reached his semi-detached, brick stone house in no time but it seemed a long one especially with a belly full of booze and Valium not to mention heroin. In the house I knew was a whole alternative system. A misunderstood community of junkies bumming kicks and living from one fix to the next. Injecting the narcotics is really the key to this community however I have never fancied the level of dedication and sacrifice required for acceptance. *It doesn't sound much of a kick to me,* I thought. *But why so many drop outs?* I ponder briefly.

My mind, through its anesthetised state, gave feeling of apprehension and caution. There is no time to re-evaluate my thought, with Cabin leading the way we arrived instantaneous and I was walking in the house. I was in a very drugged induced state and more than mildly drunk from those ill thought-out pints of Guinness that I greedily drank for no particular reason other than to feel swell… more so swell.

The house looked relatively normal from the exterior minus the disregarded garden on the front, an anomaly with the rest of the street. The windows were entirely covered with what looked like an assortment of cloths, sheets and stuck to the window itself was this "A Vampires Den" mural. An interesting analogy I thought if that was indeed its purpose to provoke thought.

I step in to the hall way, a flight of stairs where to my left, a corridor to other the rooms to my right. The carpet seemed to have an elaborate pattern of paisley although through lack of care, the patterns seemed to twist and morph into markings unintelligible and the soles of my shoes seemed to stick to the surface – no more a carpet but a used sanitary towel.

'There is no need to take your shoes off, my mate,' Cabin said.

'Thank fuck,' I whispered under my breath.

We made our way down the corridor to our right and we stopped in the kitchen. Over flowing sharps bins stacked full of used needles lay open on the kitchen unit. Charred spoons left waiting to be cleaned; bottle tops, an over flowing bin made up of empty bottles of booze, used pins lay obsolete on the counter, a set of scales and two bags of what looked like junk were in my field of vision. I accidently kicked an empty bowl on the floor crusted with dried up dog food. No actual food in site. The kitchen was what looked to me like organised chaos. We stopped in the kitchen. Cabin asked me if I would care to shot a whiskey. I declined. I wanted drugs. I was concerned only with the two packages on the counter.

A pleasantly soft, sexy voice interrupted my ogling.

'Hey there, you coming in?' asked a lady sat over in the sitting room.

I looked over; she was sitting, poised in the lotus position in front of some trinkets. I said hello and asked how she was. I was a bit taken back. The kitchen opened up into a larger room. The room was dimly lit causing a certain ambience. There was two worn out, old styled settees, a few cabinets full of crap and a record player with decent looking speakers and sat in the middle of the room was a hot young chic. Despite all the atmospherical disturbance, this cat radiated some sexual energy not usually felt when on junk. Perhaps the booze and Valium were to blame? Or was this girl electrifying?

She was sat crossed legged so from what I could tell, she was wearing a white, baggy, long sleeved T-shirt, probably stolen from an ex-lover, with the 'Aladdin Sane' Bowie cover design printed on it. The sleeves were tarnished by speckles of blood presumably from shooting. It still looked good on her. Between her legs, no light shone but if the light was to shift, one would see all. She looked early twenties in age. Her hair looked in need of shampoo but it was tied up and appeared nice enough. Her hair colour was brunette, note "I love brunettes – fuck yes"! I walked closer and her piercing eyes met mine. She asked if I would like a fix in a slow drawl. I said yes but she was already preparing a fix.

Cabin proclaimed loud and with authority, 'Ah, kid here [slaps me on my back hard], is going to stash our stuff for us and in return we are going to treat him like royalty and fix him up. He's a fiend alright – no offense lad, aren't we all, eh? So, he can help us (slaps my back again, this time like chums)!'

'We're mates me and thee, met his down the "Owd" toad nodding like a new born baby he was.'

'Think about it for a second while our lady cooks us all up a shot. It's best to ponder thoughts when fixed right Josh?'

'I guess,' I replied, 'no harm in weighing things up proper like.'

We sat in a trio eyeing the brown liquid drawing into each syringe. The smell of vinegar is wonderful. What a graceful sight to behold. Mesmerising like staring into a fire until it dances a dance in front of you.

This proposal of stashing junk is certainly not what I had in mind but it's better than sucking Cabin's cock. Man, I'd rather fuck that junky bird sat there though dude to be honest. My sexual urges take control and I lose ability to rationalise. I confirm that it was indeed my assignment to stash said drugs and so she invited me to sit next to her on a pillow. The trinkets in front of her was a metal hypodermic syringe, a bottle cap full of dissolved heroin with a cigarette filter sat in the junk, a CD case in which lay rocks of powdered brown dope. Lay at the opposite side of the CD case was a large pile of high-quality cocaine – fish scale it is called due to its resemblance. The sight was irresistible. My mouth watered and excitement overcome any high I was experiencing. My cock hardened. Before walking toward her, I tucked my blood filed penis up into my pocket.

My very movement in doing so prompted her to say, 'You needn't tuck your cock away, mate, my cunt is quite visible.'

I paused for a moment. I could see her fanny lips spread open in the position she was sat. But she turned the conversation on to the drugs she was preparing. Legs still spread my cock hard and sticking out my trouser fly. She giggled and looked at my cock. She bit her lip and breathed heavy. She whispered to me as cabin went for more whisky, 'I'm going to fix you and fuck you, babe.'

She stroked the tip of my cock and licked up some pre-ejaculation that had oozed its way out due to her sexual advances. She seemed to enjoy its taste and swallowed it with no qualms.

'What's your name?' I ask her.

'Call me Lou babes and I already know you sweetheart; I've already tasted you.'

She used her hypodermic syringe to draw up a certain amount of heroin then drew up a similar amount of liquid cocaine. I sat on a pillow next to her.

'I usually snort my gear,' I say.

'Not in here we don't,' she said. 'Shooting is the best. Right in the main line! Try it!' I'm sitting here very fucking curious. I say nothing and she picks up on my vibrations.

'Man, I'll shoot it for you... a speedball I've just fixed it up especially for you babe.'

Giving me a wink and a pull on my cock. I have only ever snorted a speedball, many times too, I suppose it all enters the blood so to hell with the route of administrations. She tourniquets my arm tight and begins to find a suitable vein. I twitch with anticipation and excitement. I was faintly aware of the transaction taking place but my self-control was diminished, I could not help myself. Her sexual advances and with the promise of hard narcotics is far too heavy man. What the hell, it's my final shot, last blow out. Enjoy it while it lasts. I'm a sucker for pleasure, sucker for relief.

'Hit me Lou, hit me hard.'

I love your enthusiasm boy, sit still and relax.'

She strokes a fat vein on my arm and she pulls back the plunger filled with junk, coke and blood then she hits the plunger back into my vein knowing she has hit a bull's eye.

Chapter 8
"My Final Hit with Sister Morphine"

Cabin comes back into the room with a bottle of whiskey and three glasses just as Lou was hitting me with the shot. He looked over and shared his dismay that I should get the shot first. Lou retorted, 'Shut the fuck up Cabin, you've had plenty for now. Drink some whiskey and eat some goof balls, that will get you going.'

'What you think I'm doing? Checking the fucking sell by date?'

He scoffs and turns away.

'Ignore him babe, you enjoy this and the moment she shoots and takes the pin out of my arm, a flood of synapses sending pleasure, energy, vitality and warmth overwhelms my senses from head to toe. I lay back next to Lou as she prepares her fix, well it's what I think she's doing. She intermittently flops my limped cock around and sucked the tip of penis hungry for more discharge.

She need not bother, my world is complete, inhibitions dissolved, egos taken a hike and the hole in my heart, the pain that goes with it is filled and relieved. I breathe a deep breath in and out.

Oh, what pleasure. This cat has hit me good. The flow of cocaine pulsing around my system in tandem with the heroin is exhilarating beyond belief and few words could describe it other than complete and utter euphoria. The elixir of life and death I mutter.

'Speedballs are dangerous. You know that you're in deep when this is your daily routine. It's a game of Russian roulette and boy, if the heart gives out, death! Too much dope in there and you stop breathing – death. You buy your ticket and take the ride.'

This was Cabin's input but I am far too high to bother. I have no worries in the world right now. Wouldn't you, reader? Of course, Cabin speaks the truth even if he doesn't follow the protocol himself. This shot's strong. I'm trying to not pass out in fear of being raped or fucked over.

So, I stand up slowly and lean on the kitchen table. There is a pack of smokes on the counter and a lighter, I don't usually dig tobacco but what is it like now? I should like to try one. I call to Lou asking whose cigarettes are on the kitchen top.

'Mine,' she says, 'take one babe.'

'You're an archangel Lou.'

No bother J (my newly acquired nickname "J" far better than ginge eh?) so I take the smoke, light it and take a moderate toke on the Embassy N01 Fag. Steady as she goes, don't want to puke. Lou slowly walked my way after her shot. She seemed composed however a glow happened to be surrounding her. Colour returned to her skin especially her face. She was hot and reeked of sexual desire.

Now now Josh, remember your fiancé I think to myself with difficulty. I've got to get out of here before I bed this lady of the night and finish up with kilos of cabins brown to stash at ours which is definitely not fucking happening. I must plan an exit strategy.

Lou leans up against me and kisses my forehead while taking the cigarette and toking big bellows of smoke from it shortening its length considerably.

'Smoking is nasty J,' she says softly spoken, her hit obviously taking affect. 'It doesn't suit you babe. I'm going to fuck you later J. Mark my words.'

My dick twinges and stiffens slightly again. She notices and Cabin looks on through his one eye while he's smoking what I presume to be crack from his pipe.

I doubt small talk is going to get me out of this predicament in which I find myself. Lou advances continue but she senses a hesitation from me as she cups both of my balls and the base of my shaft.

'Your wound up real tight J, why not take a little bump to get you in the groove. I tell ya, you ain't leaving here without a fucking and as for the arrangements you've made with that low life in there,' she nods over towards Cabin still inhaling leftovers of crack, 'well that's your twos business, I don't give a fucking damn.'

I get the feeling Lou gets what she wants often. She is an enchantress, bringing the worst out of me. Or have I done that to myself? Maybe a medley of the two I conclude.

'Here.'

She chirps, takes a bump of coke, puts a small silver spoon with a heap of whitish powder on it up to my face. I sniff it hard and lean back onto the kitchen unit, my head flops back with it. I can feel Lou chugging on my cock. I cannot feel much until she put it in her mouth and sucks hard.

I groan and even thrust my hips a little but something else is going on here. Was that coke on that spoon? My vision begins to fade starting from my peripheries and closing in on my entire vision. My head and chest glow hot with a rush of chemicals but something is not right. I'm losing control of my body and I begin to nod standing up while this cat blows my penis. She laughs but her voice is distant.

'Stand still,' I think she said. But I have no ability to stand, I'm merely balancing with her holding me up, cock in gob! I try to talk but I can only mumble. The euphoria turns to nothingness and as it does, both my knees buckle. I can feel myself almost in a slow motion I slide down the work surface and onto the floor. There is still a clamp around my penis and I hear muffled giggles. I pass out but I'm soon semi-conscious caused by the bickering and voices full of panic.

'That was no cocaine you bumped him with, it's the uncut horse I picked up this morning for punters. Need to add the bash yet, you stupid bitch. How much you sling him, eh?'

'Maybe a point and a half (150mg) I hear,' Lou tentatively replies sorry like. I'm defiantly lying on some cold tiling. I can see two sets of legs but each time I focus it fades. She's gone and sent me over no doubts about it. I hear Cabin bark at her loud.

'Where the fuck are we going to stash those keys our youth sent us now you've killed the twat?'

'And great!'

Cabin continues, 'We have a young ginger corpse to get rid of now. Sure as shit no ambulance is coming into the gallery. The fuzz will have a field day, for Christ's sake!

Fancy another stint withdrawing in a jail cell do you? You dopey cow!'

My vision fades again and I gasp for a breath.

'We are going to have to gather all the works and catch that cruise pronto!'

Chapter 9
Woke Up, Very Close to the Edge

The Late great Hunter S Thompson spoke about the egde in his gonzo journalistic piece "The Hells Angels". If my memory is serves me well, Dr Thompson spoke of the edge being a concept in the hells angels when riding fast and hard in a fleet of beast like chopper bikes. "The only person who know what's over the edge is those who went off it". but few are around to share what's over there was the point, past help, dead with his beautiful bike, his only true love mangled in with flesh and bone, Brain and face distorted horrifically smeared round 'the edge'.

That is a heavy digression but Dr Hunter S Thompson has been a large part of my growing up in a false and misleading society and really on the fringes of authority and law. I'll admit, I live on the fringes such society. Drugs abuse came after alcohol. Then the two combined creating a force of no direction in life. Booze never fails to create a monster or someone with dementia equally so.

I came too around six hours later. My shirt was ripped open top to bottom. I had bruise marks on my chest and ribs.

I felt so sick, Nausea racked my body and my head ached to the point of horror where ever light shone. I was in and out of a delirious episode. What was left of my shirt was covered in spilt fluids; booze, specks of blood on my sleeve and shirt collar. Vomit and some unknown sticky substance, looked like cum, in fact, it was cum no doubt about it and more specs of blood here and there on my jeans. Apart from a sucker of a hangover, the blood was certainly disconcerting, I didn't feel physically injured.

What on earth happened here? I think to myself, dread and nerves knot my stomach and I feel the need to shit. I'm beginning to withdraw too. My last shot, I presume, was last night or at best in the early hours prey. I hope to Christ I have some dope on my person even a few goof balls; Valium, Xanax even a Bromazepam. The latter is a French favourite, an analogue of Diazepam but with some differences. The word on the street is Bromazepam is stronger than its counterpart diazepam, a perfect replacement. I never got the attraction weather down to my tolerance – need a higher dose or they just weren't my bag. I felt privilege to have obtained thirty bars of them regardless. See drug addiction extends to an obsession; collecting, trying and using, abusing, mixing and matching, even recording their properties once used. It consumes you. It gets under your skin. Then there is crack cocaine.

I'm lay, propped up by my elbows and a few hip style cushions on a Persian carpet and with psychedelic throws and blankets placed over and surrounding me. It must have been daytime although miserable out. I can tell by the moth-eaten sheets covering the window. I lie back down briefly and take the ceiling watch. Blood was on the ceiling, dried blood and new. It's a common practice of the idle Junky to draw up blood after their fix and shoot the contents on walls or the ceiling. I still do not understand this practice. As if us junkies need more filth. I have seen dope fiends spray the left-over contents of a shot out of the barrel onto walls or ceilings; seen people who use speed, crack or crystal meth in their shots or alongside them and use their blood to draw pretty little childlike drawings. Sinister and horrific to witness and very disconcerting. Voodoo drawings accurately describe this artwork.

I make a plan on how to leave the gaff I am in right after scoring a morning fix to get me home to my semi healthy stash. So, I toss my soiled shirt into a corner, the smell it gave off was revolting; no amount of Daz detergent nor safety pins will revive the garment, its trash but it is certainly a nod to the punk counter-culture or too Viviane Westwood's seventies "sex" fashion collections. I choose a moderate size blanket from the nest I have been lay in and headed to the John for a morning empty. The stench of booze and drugs were like noxious fumes making me want to gag. I quickly finish up and wash my hands and face in the sink with a bar of soap. I then spray a healthy amount of Burberry Touch which was surprisingly sitting on the filthy window sill. I never got a kick from wearing Burberry Touch; smells like an unhygienic barber shop in my opinion but better than intense drug stench, vomit and cum included. I try to keep up appearances but it's difficult in this game. I wet my hair attempting to accomplish a basic style and down a few glasses of water.

Now the fundamentals are taken care of or at least to an extent, I need to fix up and work out the situation now which could have easily been a priority depending on one's level of sickness. The house I am crashing in sounds and feels desolate, cold and abandoned. It felt a bit unnerving at the time. I look round attentively.

It is bloody freezing cold, I shiver down to my bones and it's painful in a state of smack withdrawal and probably benzodiazepine dependency alongside for good measures. Opioid withdrawal is the worst. It's a curse and it rarely goes without a partner. Booze, crack, cocaine hydrochloride, speed or most often benzodiazepines. The pharmacy shit. The latter, along with some crack or coke certainly has me hooked and on my knees. So to begin with I check my pockets and I feel a familiar something in there. A wash of relief relaxes me. I must have some kind of fix tucked wisely away last night so those jackals couldn't feed on my food. Working their tricks and angles. I sniff a swift line of heroin and swallow a few Valium. I stumble out the bathroom and straight back into a bed.

Side Note

There exists numerous authorities who write extensively about the use, abuse and lifestyle of an opioid addict; Thomas De Quincey, William H Borroughs, Alaxander Trocchi and Irvine Welsh to name a few. All of which are well versed in the topic. I feel I have more to add to the subject.

Notes on the title

I have called this piece of work 'the Cruise Vacation' more out of a personal view I have on the act of going on a cruise ship. I envision a large steel tanker of a ship, spruced up but the foundations are the same as an oil tanker. A cruise ship moves from one beautiful place to another much like a narcotic does however sometimes the destination is sour and bleak. The mode of transport is ugly but dressed up beautifully. An analogy to junk and all the drugs we use to feel good. The drug is the vessel and the vessel is often ugly dressed up and glorified by the user. Hell, it even feels damn good for a while but imagine being stuck on that damn cruise liner. Sea sick, junk sick and only seeing those beautiful places from afar never quiet being able to reach them, they may as well be a dream.

Chapter 10
Drugs, Chicks and Breakfast in Bed

I am not writing this as a plagiarised version of the many stories of excess and hedonism experienced by my ideals, musical masters and authors alike. This story is mine and mine alone. From a quote on quote, "Normal junky's perspective" which can, indeed be a hard concept to explain to those who have not lived a life surrounded by pleasures, visceral and literal, the highs were pleasurable beyond belief, alone slumped on a coach and then there's the lowest low. Pain; hellish and nauseating beyond belief.

Nauseating like waking up to the smell of cheap tobacco being burnt and smoked while I kip. It woke me straight up, my stomach churns and I feel as though my arteries are clogging with plaque, remnants of narcotics building up and the smoke leaving me with an approximate fifty-fifty ratio of oxygen and carcinogens. I open my eyes to a blinding sting as the smoke engulfs me, obscuring my vision. That overly sweet stench of the cheap tobacco smoke drifts its way past me and permeating its way through my pillow; acting as a fucking filter as the thick smoke finally escapes and drifts majestically through the crack in the damp bay window. I watch it disperse in the cold winter's morning. I could throw up any minute; my mouth waters and I gag but I manage to swallow the vile tasting vomit before I mess whoever's bed sheets I am occupying. I'm lying in bed in a scarcely decorated room, the odd nick knack here and there. The walls were damp and flecks of off-white paint looks to be falling from the neglected walls. I groan with painful annoyance, turn over to hang off the right side of the bed and assess what is on the menu for breakfast, a hypodermic syringe filled with hard drugs on the bed side? Unfortunately, not at present. That will need attending too pronto. I must take care of those priorities before even thinking of the day ahead. Hopefully someone's cooking up down stairs. Just a glass of water sits on a bed side table and a goof ball lay behind a picture frame. Looks like a donkey chocking Halcion which I sincerely appreciate. Left by whom I'm unsure, I'm yet to turn over and acknowledge the smoker in the room. I must thank them, priorities first though Joshua, I need to fix up and feed that junk gouging gorilla stuck on my back if you catch my drift. I stretch and reach for the pill and by Christ, I realise I am not alone in the bed itself, there is internal movement in the duvet for sure, I can feel it as my leg touches someone I hope to be a woman. My stomach drops again with mounting anxiety.

A brunette chick is sitting up next to me smoking the straight Embassy cigarette that has got me up so pettily annoyed. Symptoms of my developing withdrawals no doubt. Growing, grown and growing some more. I must fix up to avoid shitting the bed for a start I think to myself. Face glows red and I hold in a look of embarrassment at my brittle state. Too young to be in such a physical mess man. *'I need to get wise and clean up my act'* I think to myself. I sneakily let out a fart of noxious fumes into my boxer shorts. Boxers? I questioned how was I in boxers. Where are my threads, chick? And my shirt? I'm in me kecks here babe, I verbally realise, that fucking Halcion takes your mind on a walk, ability to deal with day-to-day crisis gone and I think on or try too at least.

She giggles really cute like, she's a very radiant woman, like untouched, unmarked and gentle. If I was to guess I would say she was in her late twenties. Must have got away with that fart I snuck out. Chick of this calibre is not going to care much for such pig antics, I've got to play this smooth as far as my body allows. I ask her if she minds me snorting a couple of bumps of heroin in her presence, not knowing how on earth she might react to such a question. I want to avoid explaining it to firm up my bowels because this cat doesn't look like a dope head.

She just giggles and says, 'I fixed up before you woke, sweety, who am I to deprive a sick man of his medicine?' she asks rhetorically.

'Right on, thank you,' I said sheepishly and rather surprised but I really shouldn't be. These Opioids whether the shit is Codeine; Dihydrocodeine, Oxycodone, Heroin or Fentanyl and the many analogues are plaguing every street and subsequently a vast majority of homes in western civilisation alone.

She replied, 'No worries.'

All Jolly and chirpy.

'Can I get you anything to help you fix up babe?'

I think back to my experience hitting a vein last night, I contemplate that route, just a last second dig but for once, mindfulness prevailed over my addiction so I asked for a book and if there is any possibility of selling me some junk and maybe a few more Halcion if she indeed gave me the first. She had and she was more than content at setting me up with five more pills and the largest collective amount of Heroin I have ever seen stored in an ounce zip lock baggie, the ones you can buy your lids of weed in. Although going by the rocks and powder in this bag, its notable weight and by the visible way it bulged out once held aloft, I would have predicted at least a few ounces in that bag if not double more. The amount I debagged to use left no noticeable dent in the bag put it that way. At the time it felt unreal, magical man. I have enough dope to last half a year at least being fucking optimistic with that approximation but still. What a score.

I was extremely excited to the point I struggled to contain myself. She just handed it me casually and in there I saw a small silver point of a gram spoon. A point is a usual dose of heroin for a human – around seventy to eighty milligrams to a point for a first timer or someone with smaller body mass index. It starts that way and escalates until you can easily triple that amount and remain on earth.

'Here, knock yourself out,' she said followed by, 'but don't.'

Which reeked of sexual suggestion especially in combination with her sexual energy given off as she lay down beside me, rolling onto her front and kicking back her legs then intertwines them. She's wearing sun kissed tights, feet on show. I have a hard on with evident discharge most definitely crusted on my black Calvin's. Should have worn white boxers in hind sight but I wasn't to know, was I? I can't predict the future. Maybe prepare better is next year's new resolution along with kicking the junk. The hard on was initially caused by junk withdrawal. It will do that to a dude. Welcome back wet dreams but they are far from pleasant I assure you. Senses go into over drive. Bodily fluids from tears to cum discharge will most certainly begin exiting the body with haste. I need some dope fast. I think past cooking any up for now that takes a minute and my senses are sharp enough I just cannot hold on. I need fast action here. Roll up a note on the double.

I quickly get over the shock of the situation and unzip the sandwich bag of smack. Some dust remnants cloud from the bag and I immediately smell vinegar and a floral scent of quality dope which alone smoothens some of life's sharper edges already. The body's senses a fix viscerally. I take the spoon and have a field day. Spoon after spoon until I was nodding, head flopping all over the fucking place.

I used the book Naked Lunch which I couldn't figure out if it was simply just ironic or the lush was fucking with my head which I couldn't be doing with at all, four lines of dope, two for each nostril, just for the novelty like. Zooming past the brink of no return which might subsequently end in me asking for her to shoot it me intravenously. I for some stupid reason, still associate snorting junk as being the healthy way to smack up. I remind myself; we are all in the same boat, pal. I go to hand the sandwich bag of heroin back however the lass refuses says that its mine for home. Cabin's fucking stash of course. Shit! I thought I'd get out of here without this shit and all for forty mother's little helpers and an intravenous hit of a speed ball. Seemed damn worth it at the time. Man, that hit was really nice. It put me on the edge. Seems I didn't fall off of the proverbial edge this time though thank fuck. I'll scheme up a false address and not be seen in these parts again that's for sure.

I'll have no need for any road. That bag of smack will keep me going until the Christmas cheers are over and I'm going turkey in the new year. The last few years have been hell on Christmas. I am not religious, spiritual maybe but this Christmas shite is a commercial power house. It's driven by the rich to take from the poor. Have two kids with an average paid income times two and you're still fucked. The children will want a new gaming computer, PlayStation, whatever and goods the big wigs worldwide are advertising and of course the kids have seen the adverts that's for fucking sure. It's a messy system but I do appreciate family time especially without screaming kids wanting those god forsaken gifts Santa neglected to drop off. I don't know why I'm so cynical of the whole affair. I benefitted gratefully since a child at Christmas. The Junkies blues I guess, beat and cold. Old before my time. I think walking the balance between high or sick in front of family was very difficult and for the most part I was unsuccessful.

I got those few more Halcion off Lou for flicking her bean off until she squirted sex juices and piss over her duvet. She's a dirty little moggy cat that's for sure. Her conservative looks and her behaviour whether sexual or playing fucking mind games is mind blowing to say the least. Great times. But my girl. What a hopeless set up, man. But I get told often that these games are only business but shit can easily go far out. Look at this rather beautiful looking birdie lying alongside me with blaring disdained wonder – again rather paradoxical, a common accord in the junk trade one will find. She must be able to read my state or at least my uninviting facial expressions.

'Don't worry, sweet cheeks, nothing happened last night.'

Relief washes over me.

'You passed out downstairs and Cabin and Drew had to drag you up here to sleep.'

I rub my face and ruffle up my hair.

'So, where am I?' I asked hoping for something like 'Your own bed, silly,' something Jenny would say but that's fantasy at this point in time.

'You're in Hyson green babe.' Lou replied as she blew out another bellow of poisonous smoke. I cough and hope I have an inhaler for my asthma although this junk has slowed my breathing so good it isn't an issue no more. Watching this innocent appearing cat lying in bed in a suggestive position, smoking made my groin pulsate. I'm horny and through the junk haze and hangover too. The smack creeps up my body like a warm soft cashmere coat. This is the plane of existence where things happen.

'I thought you were dead for a while. I gave you the kiss of life. You overdosed last night… what's your name? Joe?'

'Josh,' I replied looking around the room distracted and smacked out.

The junk is in control now. No problemo. Even the room looks cosy.

'You were very poorly, you know, you need to be careful.'

She instructed in a serious tone of voice. I try and make some sense of things but it's difficult. I notice a bowl of vomit lay on the floor next to the bed.

'Is this your gaff?' I asked her.

She sat and observed my confusion. My speech slurred half caring where I was by now.

'No, it's this guy's place. Davie he's called. He's a cool cat, lets people shoot up and smoke in here away from the street if you pull him a favour or two you know. You met Cabin in the boozer down the road, the old toad. He noticed you nodding away in the corner of the pub. Sleeping like a new born he said. He sold you some goof balls I think. You bought a lot off him. Perhaps it explains why the over dose.'

'Have you got a habit then like with a proper yen for the gear?' she asked quizzically.

'Yeah.'

I nodded with a crooked smile.

'And with a bastard of a high tolerance too due to me sniffing the shit.'

'I feel you boyo!' she replies sounding understanding.

'So your full blown and stuck with a habit.'

She confirmed without the need of an answer from me.

'Well now, hasn't Josh been a naughty boy, eh?'

She asked if I would like a hit cooked up this time. I was still dizzy and nauseous from last night's apparent overdose and todays OD in progress.

'Perhaps not, you were a mess last night chick and you've only just sniffed a lot too.'

'I'll be even more of a mess if I don't fix up soon though, love.'

I looked up at her as if she had all the answers in the world while attempting to conceal my already smacked up state. I just wanted more. She looked at me, ruffled my hair and placed her hand on my cheek.

'You a mess kid.' she says in a motherly fashion.

Fat bag of heroin resealed and lay next to each other's thin now naked bodies. Sexual stimulation to its core, smack and fanny laid out like a fucking buffet. What a killer. I ask in an exaggerated posh English accent.

'Might you have any cocaine to join that brown in the barrel, ma lady?'

'Yes? Yes! Fuck yes!'

She almost squeals with excitement – like she forgot a bit she had stashed in her bra or something – don't think I was far wrong too. She railed out another four lines of coke. Quality fish scale cocaine. I opt to snort it. She does too and she notably acquires vitality and energy. She was insatiable and beautiful… but not like my fiancé at home. She's a babe and I want out of here and into her arms. I want to heal the wounds I have caused.

To begin with, I must cut ties and do a runner from here. I grab the bag of smack and stash it in my rucksack to take home. They are counting on me wanting a stable supply of dope from them in the future but after taking the hefty bag of brown, I have no intention of merely stashing it for them. So, I jot down our previous rented apartment's address to throw them off my scent and confirmed they had my number then I handed the note to the lass in bed with sincerity and confidence.

'Just call when you need access to the dark,' I say to her with confidence brought on by the heroin.

She's happy for me to depart. The house was barren when I got down the stairs. All the junkies out on the steal or to score I surmise which suits me just fine; now I am well, good and high. Once on the street I immediately take off to the tram stop with a spring in my step though a little nervous – another

Halcion will take care of that. On the way I take the sim card with the number I had gave to them out of my phone and snap it in two. Before I did, I contacted my phone's network and requested a new number as soon as humanly possible. This could be the difference between life and death. Like keeping alive on heroin is easy I think not. Well, what's done is done. The first day of the new year I clean up my act and I vowed to myself to never return to dope and especially to the Old Toad Boozer. Easy to write, solid to achieve but achievable nonetheless.

Drug abuse, over curiosity and obsessive behaviour landed me here, from registered nurse, to junky to a qualified barber and back then clean again and so that continues. It's been quite the ride around that old block. Being an addict is one thing, being in control and clean is another. Two extreme states of being, a world apart from one another. My journey between worlds was an endurance race, a complete recalculation of the mind. A reboot with a mindfulness update. I have cleaned up and I am better for it but the journey was horrendous, and in many respects, still is. I could not have done it alone that is for damn sure. I will always be a junky, it is up to me to write about it and achieve such visceral highs without the dope and carry on, being strong and present, surfing the waves of life with the confidence to be me, to find my real place in the rat race that is 'society'.

The opposite is drugs and a young death, "Live fast, die young, leave a beautiful corpse," suggested Jim Morrison of the Doors. Live life instructed by the Greek God of the Vine Dionysus and follow Miss Joplin's advice, "if it feels good, do it".

I do know, drugs are absolutely everywhere and once one has felt the delights on offer, one soon forgets the pain, you'll always sniff out drug suppliers wherever you reside and the pleasure of the elixir is remembered oh so fondly. The danger not so much. I keep my guard up, never letting it down.